JACOB'S
SCHOOL PLAY
STARRING HE, SHE, AND THEY

Fountaindale Public Library District
300 W. Briarcliff Rd.
Bolingbrook, IL 60440

BY IAN & SARAH HOFFMAN
ILLUSTRATED BY CHRIS CASE

MAGINATION PRESS • WASHINGTON, DC • AMERICAN PSYCHOLOGICAL ASSOCIATION

For everyone who stays true to themselves. Especially Calder, who leads by example—IH & SH

To OC and all of the residents of Sunset Sea. Especially Bob—CC

Magination Press

Books for Kids From the
American Psychological Association

maginationpress.org

Magination Press is a registered trademark of the American Psychological Association. Order books at maginationpress.org or call 1-800-374-2721.

Book design by Rachel Ross
Printed by Phoenix Color, Hagerstown, MD

Library of Congress Cataloging-in-Publication Data
Names: Hoffman, Ian, 1962- author. | Hoffman, Sarah, author. | Case, Chris, 1976-illustrator.
Title: Jacob's school play: starring he, she, and they / by Ian & Sarah Hoffman; illustrated by Chris Case.
Description: Washington, DC: Magination Press, [2021] | "American Psychological Association." | Summary: Jacob's class learns about the use of pronouns of their own choosing when, while preparing for a school play, they learn that their non-binary and gender-fluid classmate, Ari, prefers "they."
Identifiers: LCCN 2020042554 (print) | LCCN 2020042555 (ebook) | ISBN 9781433836770 (hardcover) | ISBN 9781433836787 (ebook)
Subjects: CYAC: Gender identity—Fiction. | English language—Pronoun—Fiction. | Theater—Fiction. | Schools—Fiction.
Classification: LCC PZ7.1.H634 Jac 2021 (print) | LCC PZ7.1.H634 (ebook) | DDC [E]—dc23
LC record available at https://lccn.loc.gov/2020042554
LC ebook record available at https://lccn.loc.gov/2020042555

Manufactured in the
United States of America
10 9 8 7 6 5 4 3 2 1

Jacob and Sophie were so excited about the class play! Ms. Reeves had helped each kid pick their part. Now the classroom buzzed as everyone worked on costumes and sets.

"I'm going to build the tractor engine," said Jacob.
"And I'll get the wagon ready!" said Sophie.

"Emily, who are you in the play?" asked Jacob.

"She's the cow," interrupted Noah. "See her tail?"
Emily held a string of pom-poms.

Jacob looked at Noah, "You're the sheep, right?"

"The ram!" yelled Noah.

"Isn't a ram just a sheep?" asked Jacob.

"A ram's a boy sheep," said Emily. "See his horns?"

Across the table, Ari painted big, blue swirls.

"Who are you in the play?" asked Jacob.

"Water," said Ari.

"Which water?" asked Jacob. "Are you the cloud, the rain, or the pond?"

"Yes," Ari nodded. "I'm the water."

Jacob frowned. "Ms. Reeves, why does Ari get to play three parts?"

"They don't have three, just one—the water," said Ms. Reeves.

Jacob looked at Sophie. She shrugged.

Noah tested the glue, strapped on his horns, and ran headfirst into Ari.

"Stop it!" shouted Ari.

"What happened?" asked Ms. Reeves.
"He butted him!" said Jacob.

"I'm not *him*," said Ari. "I'm *they*."
"Ari, you're just one kid," said Noah.

"*They* means two kids." said Jacob.
"*They* can mean one kid," said Ari.

Jacob dipped his brush into a tub of green paint and thought: Ari was water. The water in the play was three things. Was that why Ari was *they,* instead of *he* or *she*?

"Ari, are you a boy or a girl?" asked Jacob.

"There's more than just boy and girl," said Ari.

Jacob switched to black paint as he worked on the tractor wheels. "You could be a boy or a girl and still wear whatever you want. I do. Sophie does."

"So do I," nodded Ari, adding ribbons to their cardboard cloud.

Jacob painted and thought some more.

Ms. Reeves sat down next to Jacob.

"Are you confused about Ari?"

Jacob nodded.

"Well, some kids feel like boys. Some kids feel like girls.
And some kids feel like both—or neither.
In our classroom, we say *he, she,* or *they* when we talk
about people."

"But boys can wear dresses," said Jacob, "and be *he.*"

"That's right, but that's different," said Ms. Reeves. "This isn't about what you wear. This is about who you are. Inside."

"Who is Ari, inside?" asked Jacob.

"From the outside, we can't see who *anybody* is on the inside," said Ms. Reeves. "So we have to trust them when they tell us."

A week later, the classroom echoed with happy chatter as family and friends found seats for the play.

Ms. Reeves turned out the lights and the room went quiet.
She flipped the lights back on, and the sun stepped through the door.
"I'm up!"

Farmer Sophie stepped out of the barn and breathed in deep.

"I love the smell of sunshine," she said. The whole room chuckled.
"Let's plant some corn!"

Jacob rode the tractor out of the barn. "I've got the corn kernels!"
"Time to go in the dirt," said Sophie. She tapped each kernel gently.
Snug in the dirt, the kernels hummed a quiet, underground song.

Ari walked in and blocked the sun.

"Looks like rain," said Jacob.

"Good, our farm needs water,"
said Sophie.

Ari crossed the sky and
rained down on the farm.

The kernels rustled their new leaves and sang a bright, growing song.

Ari traveled to the barn, where they filled the pond.

"Moo," said Emily, walking out of the barn. "I'm glad the pond is filled."

"Baa," said Noah. "Maybe you should take a bath. You're stinky!"

"You're a rude ram!" said Emily, and chased Noah around the pond. Everyone in the audience laughed.

Trailing rain drops, Ari stood up.

Ari traveled back across the field, sprinkling rain on the corn again.

The corn stretched and sang a happy, all-grown-up song.

"Ready to harvest!" said Sophie.

Jacob stood on stage and looked at his classmates. They looked so different wearing their costumes, playing their parts. But he still knew who they were.

Suddenly, Jacob realized everyone was looking at him. It was his turn to speak, but he couldn't remember his line! So, he said what he was thinking.

"Our class is just like a farm. We all help each other grow, and everyone grows up to be what they're supposed to be. Everybody in their own way."

After Farmer Sophie had gathered up the corn, she joined Farmer Jacob and the rest of the cast in a line across the stage.
They all held hands and bowed. The audience clapped and cheered.

Jacob whispered to Ms. Reeves, "I'm glad Ari's they."
"Why's that?" she whispered back.
Jacob smiled. "Because they know who they are."

Applause filled the room, and the kids bowed again.
He, she, and they.